Growing Up Daisy

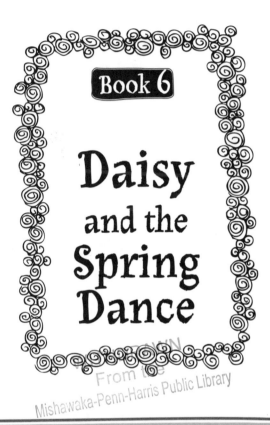

Book 6

Daisy
and the
Spring
Dance

By: Marci Peschke
Illustrated by: M.H. Pilz

Mishawaka-Penn-Harris
Public Library
Mishawaka, Indiana

visit us at www.abdopublishing.com

To Para Mis Amigas: Gerrie, Trish & Kara - MP
For Laura - MHP

Printed in the United States of America, Melrose Park, Illinois.
092010
012011
 This book contains at least 10% recycled materials.

Original text by Marci Peschke
Illustrated by M.H. Pilz
Edited by Stephanie Hedlund and Rochelle Baltzer
Cover and interior design by Abbey Fitzgerald

Library of Congress Cataloging-in-Publication Data

Peschke, M. (Marci)
  Daisy and the spring dance / by Marci Peschke ; illustrated by M.H. Pilz.
      p. cm. -- (Growing up Daisy ; bk. 6)
   ISBN 978-1-61641-119-0
   [1. Schools--Fiction. 2. Mexican Americans--Fiction.] 1. Pilz, MH, ill. 11. Title.
   PZ7.P441245Dag 2011
   [Fic]--dc22
                                    2010028457

Table of Contents

CHAPTER 1: The Boss 4

CHAPTER 2: Dance Contest.............................. 7

CHAPTER 3: Choosing a Winner..................... 16

CHAPTER 4: Committee Chaos 23

CHAPTER 5: Super Speller............................... 29

CHAPTER 6: Dress Disaster............................. 38

CHAPTER 7: Busy Bee....................................... 47

CHAPTER 8: The War 57

CHAPTER 9: Decorating Divas....................... 63

CHAPTER 10: Fourth Grade Fever................ 72

Spanish Glossary 80

1

The Boss

Blanca leaned out of the door of classroom 210 and shouted something to Daisy. It was hard to hear in the hallway of Townsend Elementary with all the kids opening and closing lockers and talking loudly.

Finally, when she was a little closer Daisy heard Blanca yell, "Hurry up! Madison says she's going to plan the Spring Dance."

Daisy sped up and dashed through the door of room 210. She was just in time to hear Madison tell everyone she was forming a committee to plan the dance.

"Do something!" Blanca whispered loudly.

Daisy put her books on her desk. Then she said, "Madison, I'm glad that you want to help with the dance. As your class president, I can use everyone's help making it a success. Just as soon as we have a theme, I'll let you know what you can do to help. Okay?"

All week Madison had been trying to take over the planning of their fourth-grade dance. Everyone knew that once Madison took charge, she took over! She liked to be the boss.

Daisy thought that everyone in the fourth grade should help plan the dance. Since all of the kids had voted for her as class president, she planned to include them all.

Raymond said, "Madison, you need to chill out. We have two whole weeks before the dance."

Madison looked like a volcano about to blow its top. "You wouldn't know anything about planning, Raymond. You do everything at the last minute!" she shrieked. Then she spun around and stomped to her desk.

Madison always thought she should be in charge. Blanca actually called her *Bossy Pants*, but not to her face.

Daisy didn't like name-calling and she really wanted to be Madison's friend. But, the more Daisy tried to be nice, the meaner Madison seemed to be.

Mami would say that Madison was just jealous, but Daisy didn't know what she could have that Madison might want. Madison had expensive clothes and traveled around the world. Daisy often wore homemade clothes and she had only been to Mexico.

Just then, their teacher breezed in. Ms. Lilly was wearing a beautiful dress with birds and bright yellow flowers all over it. She looked just like a spring garden. It was hard to believe it was already spring. That meant fourth grade was almost over!

Thinking about it made Daisy just a little bit sad. But thinking about the dance made her feel much better.

2

Dance Contest

Once Ms. Lilly was inside and all the students were seated, she said, "Good morning, my superstar students. Today I am passing out a sign-up sheet for the school spelling bee. I hope some of you superspellers will participate."

She laid a clipboard on Amber's desk. Daisy heard kids talking about the spelling bee as they passed the sheet from desk to desk. At the front of the room, Ms. Lilly had turned her back to the class and was pulling on a blue coat and something else.

Daisy tapped Blanca's arm. She gasped, "Is that a wig?" Just then Ms. Lilly spun around in a long blue coat with shiny gold buttons down the front and a white wig with long curls.

"I am a famous American," Ms. Lilly announced. "Can you guess who I am?"

Raymond seemed puzzled. Finally, he asked, "Ms. Lilly, are you a dude?"

Ms. Lilly turned and wrote on the board: *I am a dude.*

Amber raised her hand and asked if the famous American was old. Their teacher added to the board: *I am not old.*

Amber continued, "But you have white hair."

Ms. Lilly reminded the class the hair was just a wig.

Jason asked, "Are you a president?"

Ms. Lilly wrote on the board: *I am a president.* As she wrote, she said, "Very good, Jason!"

Daisy's hand shot into the air just at the same time Madison's did. Then Madison shouted, "You're George Washington!"

Ms. Lilly wrote on the board: *I am George Washington.* Then she said, "Madison, I do like your enthusiasm. But in the future, please wait until I call on you even if you know the answer to the question."

This caused Madison to immediately pout. She crossed her arms over her chest and slumped down in her chair.

Noticing this Blanca whispered, "*Madison es una bebe grande.*"

Daisy hated to agree, but Madison was acting like a big baby. Daisy said, "*¡Sí!*"

Suddenly everyone turned to look at Daisy, even Ms. Lilly. Daisy's cheeks felt red hot. She must have agreed with Blanca out loud.

"Did you say something, Daisy?" Ms. Lilly asked.

Daisy didn't know what to say. She just sputtered, "Yes, I didn't mean to though! I'm so sorry. I guess I was thinking out loud."

Some of the kids in her class laughed. Ms. Lilly was quiet for several seconds. Finally she said, "I guess it is better to think out loud than not at all. But maybe you could take notes before sharing your thoughts, Daisy."

Now Daisy felt really embarrassed. Ms. Lilly moved on to talking about the famous general George Washington. The class would be learning about the Revolutionary War.

Ms. Lilly gave them a group assignment next. They could work in groups of two, three, or four. For this assignment, they got to choose their own group members.

Daisy and Blanca turned and pushed their desks together. It was funny how they decided to work as a group without even talking about it first! Raymond looked awkwardly around the room and then pushed his desk over to theirs.

"Who asked you to join us, Raymond?" Blanca complained. Raymond looked around again and decided all the other groups were set.

He asked Daisy, "Can I please be in your group, Daisy?" Raymond knew Daisy would not say no. She was nice to everyone, even him.

Daisy told Blanca that Raymond might have some good information. Three heads are better than two she reasoned, so Blanca agreed.

Ms. Lilly gave each group a piece of paper that looked like a giant pie. Each group would brainstorm everything they knew about Washington on their pie paper. They would have fifteen minutes and Ms. Lilly was setting the timer.

Daisy laid out the pie-shaped paper on their desks. She asked, "What do we know about Washington?"

Raymond began listing things: he was the first American president, he was the general in the Revolutionary War, and he fought in the French and Indian War.

The only thing Blanca could add was that his wife was named Martha. The only thing Daisy knew about Washington was that his home was called Mount Vernon. She thought it was in Virginia, but she wasn't sure.

Looking at their list of five facts, Daisy realized that Raymond had contributed three of the five. She pointed this out to Blanca. Then she said, "Raymond, without you we would only have two things on our paper. Maybe three because I knew that he was a president."

Raymond nodded and replied, "I like history, especially the stuff about wars."

After fifteen minutes, Ms. Lilly called time to stop. Some of the groups only had one fact. Everyone knew Washington was the first president. Jason's group had ten facts. Madison's only had four.

Ms. Lilly was asking the groups to share their facts and she was writing them on the board. If a group had the same fact as another then the speaker for the group was supposed to say "stars and stripes." This was a reminder of the American flag made by Betsy Ross.

Some groups only got to say "stars and stripes." But Blanca got to say that Washington fought in the French and Indian War.

Ms. Lilly was impressed! She said enthusiastically, "Kuddos to your group, Blanca, for knowing such a superfact about our first leader."

The class moved on to an independent mini-research assignment. Ms. Lilly passed out a slip of paper to each student. The papers listed the resource each student could use. Some lucky kids got the computer. Others got encyclopedia, textbook, or library book.

Daisy got to work in her textbook, which was kind of boring, but super easy. Maybe it was a good thing. She had the assignment done in about ten minutes and Ms. Lilly had given them thirty. This gave her some time to think about the dance.

Getting out a new sheet of paper, Daisy wrote at the top: *Spring Dance*. She chewed the end of her pencil, doodled some flowers, and thought about last year's dance. But she could not think of anything that would please everyone in the fourth grade.

Blanca looked over at her paper. She grabbed the paper and wrote in big letters: HAVE A CONTEST!

"That's a great idea!" Daisy whispered.

Daisy decided to talk to Ms. Lilly and see if she could use the class bulletin board in the hall.

Then she would need to ask Principal Donaldson if she could make a morning announcement. If he agreed then tomorrow they would start the contest. It would be perfect!

Everyone in fourth grade could make a suggestion to name a theme for the Spring Dance. Then a committee with one student from each class would choose the winner. The Name Our Dance Contest was so democratic, even George Washington would approve.

3
Choosing a Winner

That night at dinner Daisy announced, "We're having a contest to name a theme for the dance. Blanca thought of the idea."

Daisy's brothers, Diego and Manuel, rolled their eyes. They wanted to talk about soccer instead. Diego grumbled, "Dances are dumb, Daisy." Manuel shouted, "Pass the rice, and I think dances are stupid, too!"

They both began chanting, "Soccer, soccer, soccer!"

Then Papi reprimanded them firmly, "Enough! We can talk about dances *and* soccer."

Abuela began to describe the dances they had when she was a young girl in Mexico.

Manuel rolled his eyes. It was a good thing Papi did not see him!

Mami sighed. She loved hearing stories about when Abuela was a girl. Daisy's younger sister Paola begged, "Abuela, tell us about your beautiful dress. *¿Que color era?*"

Abuela told them about the black skirt with the rainbow of ribbons on it with the beautiful white lace top. Daisy could tell her brothers were really bored. They had talked about dances for a long time and now it was time for soccer.

"Who has a soccer game on Saturday?" Daisy asked. Both of her brothers began to talk at once. Across the table, Papi smiled at her.

That night while she was trying to sleep, Daisy thought about a name for the dance. All she could think of was *Fun Fiesta*. She was pretty sure the rest of the kids wouldn't vote for a fiesta. It wasn't cool enough.

The next morning at school, Daisy got to make an announcement. She waited nervously in the principal's office until the bell rang. Then Principal Donaldson led them in the Pledge of Allegiance. After that, he read some announcements.

Then he added, "Now for an important announcement from our student council president, Daisy Martinez."

Principal Donaldson handed Daisy the microphone. Her throat was suddenly dry. She looked at the little pink card she had written her notes on.

She read, "Hello, fourth-grade students. You all know our spring dance is coming up, so I want to announce we are having a Name Our Dance contest. Think of a theme, make up a name for the dance, and write your idea on the bulletin board outside room 210 by Friday. We can't wait to see your great ideas and choose a winner!"

Then she quickly handed the microphone back to the principal. Whew! She was glad that was over.

Moments later she arrived in room 210. Ms. Lilly waved and asked her to take her seat. Madison gave her a smug look as she passed by. Daisy wondered if Madison had a great dance idea and would get her way after all.

Room 210 spent the morning working on their assignments about the Revolutionary War. When they finally put their books away and went to computer class, Daisy peeked at the board to see if anyone had written on it yet.

Daisy and Blanca had decorated the board that morning with white paper and sparkly red stars. Then they wrote in big blue letters *Name Our Dance Contest.* At the bottom of the board they added an envelope of blue markers.

Daisy was excited to see that two kids had left ideas. One was *Hawaiian Luau* and the other was *Square Dance Hoedown.* Those ideas seemed kind of different. Maybe she would put Fun Fiesta up there after all.

The rest of the week the board kept filling up. There were so many ideas! They included Surf's Up, Cinco de Mayo, Dancing with the Stars, Superhero Dance, Spook-tacular Ball, and Spring Fling. There was also Glow-in-the-Dark, Hollywood Red Carpet, Toon Time, Fourth Grade Fever ('70s dance), and Sadie Hawkins.

Daisy thought, *The committee will have a hard time choosing!*

The committee would have a kid from each fourth grade class on it. Madison wanted to represent Ms. Lilly's room. But since Daisy was the class president she would have to be in charge of the meeting and she would be the student representing her class.

After the bell rang Friday afternoon, DeShaye, Blair, Lucy, and Daisy all met in room 210. Madison was hanging around the door, but Ms. Lilly closed it saying, "Have a good afternoon, Madison."

The class representatives all sat at a table in the back of the room. Daisy passed out the sheets of paper she had made with all the ideas from the board.

"What are the kids in your classes saying about the kind of dance they want to have?" she asked. She didn't have to wait for a reply.

DeShaye was never shy about giving her opinion. She began with, "My class likes Toon Time and Fourth Grade Fever, but I say forget the toons. No way am I going to the dance with a bunch of guys who want to be SpongeBob SquarePants."

That got Blair's attention. He responded, "Since I'm the only guy here, I have to say that not all guys watch SpongeBob. My class likes Fourth Grade Fever, too. Our other choice was the glow-in-the-dark party."

Daisy was not sure having a dance in the dark would go over well with their principal. She thought, *Okay, so far two votes for the '70s dance.*

Daisy shared with the table that her class liked the Fourth Grade Fever idea, too. She added, "The rest of the kids in my class like the idea of the spook-tacular dance."

Lucy Chen was a friend of Min's. Min was one of Daisy's BFFs. Up until now, Lucy had been very quiet. In fact, she had not said one single thing.

Finally Lucy spoke up saying, "My class likes the disco fever dance idea. Let's go with it if you agree, Daisy."

Daisy ended the meeting very relieved to announce their dance theme was Fourth Grade Fever. It did seem to be the most popular choice after all.

4

Committee Chaos

They finally had a theme for the fourth grade dance. Now all Daisy had to do was make it happen. She knew she would need lots of help.

A lot of the fourth graders were excited to make their dance the best dance ever. But Daisy knew there would be kids who just wanted to complain.

Monday at lunch, DeShaye told her that already a few kids in her class might not come to the dance. They wanted to have a cartoon dance and didn't like the '70s idea.

In class that afternoon, Ms. Lilly was talking about the spelling bee again. Blanca rolled her eyes and hissed, "Who even wants to be in the spelling bee?"

Just then Raymond raised his hand. Ms. Lilly said, "Raymond will represent our class in the schoolwide spelling bee."

Ms. Lilly's eyes crinkled with surprise behind her glasses. Then she smiled and Daisy knew she was pleased that Raymond volunteered.

Daisy and Blanca spun around to look back at Raymond. Blanca asked, "Really, Raymond?"

Raymond just shrugged, looking a little uncomfortable. Then he said, "Sure. Why not?"

Daisy reminded him that he usually asked her to spell words for him. Raymond answered that he would just have to study a lot to get ready for the competition.

What Raymond didn't say was that he asked Daisy how to spell words so he could talk to her. He was actually a terrific speller. Ms. Lilly passed a book of words down their row for Raymond to practice with.

Daisy looked at it before she handed it to Raymond. The words inside were really long and hard to spell. Daisy was worried that Raymond would crash and burn in front of the whole school.

"I can help you practice the words after school, Raymond," she offered.

Raymond grinned and said, "Yeah, I do need some help getting ready, I guess." Really he was thinking that the spelling bee was the best thing he'd ever decided to do! Now he could spend more time with Daisy. It was working out great!

Daisy turned her attention to her committee lists. She was deciding what the other students would be best at helping with. Daisy decided she would put both Blanca and Raymond in charge of decorations.

Some of the other committees would work on refreshments, entertainment, and publicity. Madison had creative ideas, so she wrote her name under publicity. Then, Daisy put Madison's best friend, Lizzie, on the same committee. They always liked to be together.

That afternoon when Daisy got home, Abuela was making a snack. Her brothers were arguing over who would get the first plate. It was delicious melon sprinkled with chilé.

Yum! Daisy reached over Manuel's head and grabbed the plate just as Abuela began to pass it.

Manuel shouted, "Hey, no fair!" Diego complained too, but Daisy didn't even turn around. She got right to work making more committee lists.

She had not even started her homework when Blanca called. The note she made as a homework reminder was still tucked in her notebook.

As soon as Daisy answered, Blanca asked, "Did you stay and help Raymond study his spelling words?"

Daisy groaned, "No, I forgot! I hope he won't be mad at me." Tired of talking about spelling, the girls chatted about the dance until dinnertime.

Daisy was almost done making the committee lists. She decided she would post them outside room 210 the next day. She put Min, Lucy, Amber, and Genny on the refreshments committee. They all liked to make treats and would plan a tasty menu for the party. Besides, Genny made the best chocolatey good cupcakes ever!

For the entertainment committee, she chose several boys who had formed a rock band and some students who took music lessons before school. Jason could be in charge of this committee. He played guitar and was the leader of the band.

She hated to do it, but she put Madison in charge of publicity. Madison would insist on being in charge anyway. Finally she put DeShaye on the publicity committee. It was a risky decision, since Madison and DeShaye would probably argue a lot, but both would be great at publicity.

The next day, Daisy posted the list. Soon, her friends were beyond crazy. Amber didn't want to work on refreshments since she already had an idea for decorations. One of the band boys wanted to be on the publicity committee because he liked Madison.

Daisy could have cried. All of her planning was in total chaos. Finally after hearing them argue and beg her to move them around, she gave in and posted a sign-up sheet.

Super Speller

The next day after school, Daisy helped Raymond practice his spelling words for the school spelling bee. They practiced in Ms. Lilly's room.

Daisy called out the word and then Raymond could ask for a sentence or just spell the word. At first the words were pretty easy, but then they got to the words that Daisy had seen in the practice book. Words like *metamorphosis, syncopation,* and *ubiquitous*.

Daisy wondered how in the world they could ever practice enough for Raymond to do well the day of the spelling bee.

She announced, "Raymond, we better practice every day this week after school."

Raymond smiled. Then he agreed, "I know I need to practice, so I'll stay late every day."

Something about the way he smiled made Daisy nervous. Blanca was always saying that Raymond liked her, but Daisy didn't really believe it. Still, he was acting kind of weird.

They spent about thirty minutes with the spelling bee word book. Then they went to the auditorium to work on dance decorations.

Blanca and Amber were already busy making the disco balls. They were gluing squares of tin foil onto plastic balls they got at the dollar store. Amber spun a disco ball around in the palm of her hand. She bragged, "See, sparkly!"

"They are sparkly," Blanca agreed, "but gluing all of these tiny pieces is taking forever! We need help."

Raymond sat right down and got busy gluing. Daisy peeked out the auditorium door just in time to see Madison, Lizzie, and DeShaye putting up posters for the dance.

Daisy was having trouble believing what she was seeing. After all, just the day before Madison and DeShaye were about to knock each other out. Today they looked like BFFs, or at least fast friends.

"Those posters look far out!" Daisy shouted down the hall. "I can dig it." Madison almost smiled.

DeShaye shouted back, "Girl, these posters are groovy!"

Just then Genny came around the corner tossing her backpack over her shoulder. Daisy called out to Genny. She quickly explained about the difficulty making the disco balls and asked Genny to stay and help. Genny was glad to lend a hand.

Then Daisy turned to look down the other hall. She saw Jason and asked him to help, too. The work went much faster with six kids putting decorations together instead of just two.

The girls talked about their dresses and the guys talked about the band. Jason told

Raymond that his band was trying out some new songs from the '70s.

Soon Daisy announced, "It's almost five o'clock. I think we better pack up our supplies."

"Aren't you and Raymond going to practice spelling words?" Blanca asked. Then she giggled. Daisy's face got warm and pink.

Thankfully, Raymond seemed not to notice. Daisy whispered, "We already practiced. Stop teasing me about Raymond. *Estas loco* if you think he likes me."

Blanca blinked and she seemed speechless at first. "I'm sorry, Daisy. I didn't mean anything. Really!" she murmured.

Daisy smiled and warned Blanca not to pick on her anymore. Then they both laughed. Daisy felt better until Raymond shouted, "Hey, Daisy, I'll call you tonight and we can practice some more on the phone."

Blanca tried hard not giggle, but ended up making an odd snorting sound. At first Daisy wanted to say no, but then she remembered how hard some of the words were.

"I guess it's okay," she mused, "but be sure that you call after dinner."

That night after dinner, Daisy went to her room to do her homework. After she spread all of her papers on her desk, she dug in her backpack for her fuzzy pencil with the butterfly eraser. Just as she was about to get started on her math assignment the phone rang.

Manuel hollered, "Daisy, telephone! It's a boy. Is he your boyfriend?"

Diego began to chant, "Daisy has a boyfriend! Daisy has a boyfriend!"

Then Abuela scolded them saying, *"Dejen en paz su hermana."*

Daisy ran to the kitchen to get the phone and inform her nosy brothers that it was only Raymond. She added that she was helping him with something for school.

Diego's eyes twinkled with mischief, but then they darted toward Abuela. She was giving him the look.

Daisy answered, "Hey, Raymond."

"Was someone talking about me?" Raymond asked. "I thought I heard my name."

Daisy explained that her brothers were calling her to the phone, but left out the whole boyfriend thing. They practiced for a long time, but Daisy still needed to do her math homework. She told Raymond she would give him one more word and then they would have to hang up.

After they said good-bye, Daisy finished her math right away. Before she fell asleep, she thought of two more terrific decorating ideas for the dance.

The rest of the week went quickly. Every night, Daisy helped Raymond and her decorating committee. On Friday, she met Raymond again to practice one last time.

Daisy had to say he seemed ready as he could *bee*! Oddly he almost never misspelled any of the words on the practice list. This made Daisy a little suspicious. Maybe Raymond hadn't really need her help after all.

As they sat at the table in the back of their classroom, Raymond pulled a brown bag out of his backpack. He insisted, "Daisy, guess what's inside."

Daisy picked up the bag. It was a little heavy and it had smudgy spots on the outside.

Daisy sniffed. It smelled like chocolate. She asked, "Is it something to eat?"

Raymond knew she loved to eat, almost as much as he did. He said, "Yup. Chocolate chip cookies and I made them myself."

Daisy wondered if he had baked anything before or if this was his first try. She pulled out a cookie. They didn't look too dark, so they weren't burned. Never one to pass up a cookie, Daisy took a bite—or she tried to anyway. Raymond's cookies were as hard as bricks.

"I made them for you because you helped me for the spelling bee. Are they good?" Raymond asked hopefully.

Daisy just couldn't hurt his feelings after he had worked so hard. "They're good, but they would be much better with milk," she admitted. "Cookies and milk just go together."

Tucking the cookie back in the bag, she smiled at Raymond. Then she gave him one last word to spell: *chrysanthemum.* He sat pondering the word for a moment. Daisy thought it was the hardest one of all.

One by one Raymond began to call out the letters in perfect order and then at the end triumphantly said *chrysanthemum.*

Ms. Lilly, who had been very quietly working at her desk, broke into applause. She shouted, "Bravo, Raymond!"

Daisy was a little astonished. She sputtered, "Wow, Raymond, that was awesome! I think you might win!"

Raymond grinned shyly saying, "Thanks to you, I will."

Then they both headed off to the auditorium to help with decorating again. Daisy was thinking about her dress for the dance for the hundredth time. She was thinking about a long dress. Maybe a pretty purple color . . .

6

Dress Disaster

Bright and early Saturday morning, Daisy sat up and stretched. Mami and Abuela were going to start making her new dress for the dance today.

Daisy was worried. Instead of the dress of her dreams, she was getting a dress disaster. The night before Daisy, Mami, and Abuela had talked about her dress.

"Can you make a long purple dress?" Daisy had asked Abuela.

"That sounds very plain, *mi ja*," Abuela said. Then she suggested a black skirt with the rainbow of ribbons and a beautiful white lace top. It would be great for dancing in a festival, but not a disco!

Daisy gave her mother a look that said *Help*! Mami mentioned a fabric sale to distract Abuela. It seemed to work, especially when her brothers began fighting over the last piece of pizza.

Daisy had been so upset, she had even called Blanca. Her BFF advised her not to come in a folk dress. *Duh!* Everyone would tease her. The problem was that she didn't want to upset Abuela. Her grandmother did so many nice things for her.

As Daisy got dressed, she reminded herself that it was only a dress. Downstairs Mami had juice, milk, and cinnamon *pan dulce* on the table. Grabbing some sweet bread and a glass of milk, she sat down by Paola.

Soon, Mami called Daisy and Paola. She asked, "Are you ready to go shopping? Where is your abuela?"

Paola pointed out the window at the van. Abuela was standing beside it with her big, brown purse waiting for them. She was always up when the sky was still inky black. She liked to see the sun kiss the day and drink strong coffee.

Daisy knew she had probably been awake half the night designing the dress in her mind. Abuela did not need a pattern. Once she thought of a design, she laid out the fabric and cut the pieces. It was magic the way the pieces all fit together to make something wonderful. Only this time Daisy was afraid her idea of wonderful was not the same as her abuela's.

The Martinez women loaded into the van and headed off for Fabric World. Carmen was the only girl left behind with Papi, but she was just a baby.

On the way, Abuela revealed that her plan was for a long dress. It was going to be black with rainbow-colored ribbons. Daisy was thinking all she needed was the white top and she would look just like her abuela had fifty years before. She sighed.

Mami must have heard her. She said, "Abuela, let's look at the fabric before we choose a color."

Abuela said, "Sí, I like to get a sale price, especially with a long dress because it takes more material."

Daisy felt sort of relieved. At least after their shopping at Fabric World, they would go to mall for shoes and then out for lunch. It would be a fun day, even if her dress was a disaster.

Fabric World was gigantic. Mami warned Paola not to get lost and to stay close to her.

Abuela said, "She can stay by me. Come here, mi ja." Then Abuela pulled Paola along looking at fabric. That gave Daisy a chance to talk to Mami alone.

"I don't want to hurt Abuela's feelings," Daisy quietly said, "but I don't want a black dress with ribbons. What can I do?"

Mami was thoughtful. "We will have to compromise, *mi amor*. Besides, maybe it will turn out better than you think."

She winked at Daisy and held up some material that was so ugly it looked like it came from the dump. "You could be wearing this!" she teased.

Then Mami and Daisy came up with a plan that would please Abuela, but also allow Daisy to get a dress she would like. It might even turn out more fab than a purple dress.

Soon they met Abuela in the middle of the store. In her cart she had black, black, and black fabric. In Mami's cart the material was purple, white, and even one swirly, colorful print.

Mami and Daisy looked at Abuela's face. Her mouth was making a straight line and that was her stubborn face. Mami quickly pulled out the white gauzy muslin saying, "This material is only $1.50 a yard."

Then she added, "Can you make a dress with it?"

Suddenly Abuela's eyes twinkled. She bragged, "I can make a dress out of anything! Sí, this can work and it is a great buy, too."

Daisy wanted to dance. Mami's plan was working just like she expected it to.

Seeing the bright ribbons in the bottom of the cart, it was Daisy's turn to carry out her part of their secret plan. Pretending not to see the ribbon, she fished around in the cart for the boxes of fabric dye she picked out.

"Abuela, can we dye the fabric? I know you like beautiful colors and these are so pretty," she begged. The boxes of blue, yellow, pink, and green looked like a rainbow.

Abuela reached over to read the instructions on the box. Finally she asked, "Do you want the dress to be stripes of color?" Daisy explained the process of tie-dyeing the material.

Abuela grinned and said, *"**Bueno**, you will not have a dress like mine, but you'll be wearing a rainbow! Just like I did for my first dance."*

Daisy hugged Abuela tight. She said, "I'll have the best dress at the dance and it will be colored like a rainbow."

Abuela started to quietly sing an old folk song called "De Colores":

De colores, de colores
Se visten los campos en la primavera.
*   De colores, de colores*
Son los pajarillos que vienen de afuera.
*   De colores, de colores*
Es el arco iris que vemos lucir.

In English the words were:

In colors, in colors
The fields are dressed in the spring.
*   In colors, in colors*
Are the little birds that come from outside.
*   In colors, in colors*
Is the rainbow that we see shining.

The singing meant Abuela was especially happy. Daisy realized that after all of her worrying, everything was working out just right.

"Next stop, the mall," Mami called, jiggling the keys to the van. Paola said, "When your dress is too small, I will get to wear the rainbow."

At the mall, Daisy picked out some sandals with colorful straps that would look nice with her dress. Lunch was delicious! They ate in a restaurant in a big store. Daisy felt like a grown-up in the fancy room. This was special! She was glad they hadn't gone to the food court like Paola suggested.

Everyone was in a good mood after their morning of successful shopping. They talked about Daisy's dress while they ate. When they were done, not one of Martinez girls left a smidge of food on her plate.

It was time to head home and dye the soft muslin. Mami made them promise not to tell the boys about lunch. She warned, "You know how they like to eat. If you tell, we will never be able to shop again without your brothers tagging along and complaining about our shopping until we stop for lunch."

Daisy and Paola promised to never tell. Abuela put a finger over her lips. She was not going to say a word either.

Back at home they dyed the fabric and it did look beautiful when it dried. The rainbow colors were amazing.

Abuela's shears slipped through the fabric as she cut the pieces for Daisy's dress. Before bedtime, Daisy could see that the part of the dress that Abuela had sewn looked great. She couldn't wait to show it to Blanca, DeShaye, and Min.

The best part was that no one else would have a dress like hers. The design and the fabric were just as unique as Daisy. They were all one of a kind, just perfect.

7

Busy Bee

On Monday morning, Daisy got to school extra early to wait for Min and DeShaye. The night before she had called Blanca to tell her about her tie-dyed dress. Now she couldn't wait to tell her other friends all about it.

DeShaye was the first to arrive. Right away she said, "Hey, girl, you're here early. What's up?"

Daisy asked, "Did you get your dress for the dance?"

DeShaye described her new silver minidress. She added, "I want some silver eye shadow and a pair of boots to wear with it."

Spring was a hard time to buy boots, but Daisy remembered seeing some at a resale shop, so she told DeShaye. She hoped her friend would be able to get the boots. The eye shadow would be easy to find.

Daisy's mother only let her wear lip gloss, so makeup was out of the question. Besides she thought she didn't need it. She had beautiful cocoa-colored clear skin and long black eyelashes.

"Groovy! Those boots are going to be mine!" exclaimed DeShaye. They were all using words from the seventies. It was kind of fun.

Min came up to join them. She said, "I'm so nervous about my dress. My mother wants me to wear something traditional. I'll be the only square at the dance!"

Daisy encouraged her, "Maybe it won't be as bad as you think. My grandmother is making my dress and I thought it was going to be a big bummer, but it turned out stellar."

"Daisy, your granny is way cool!" DeShaye insisted.

Just then Blanca walked up. She said, "I'm going to have a halter dress. It's awesome!"

Then the bell rang and they scattered and headed for their classrooms. In room 210, Ms. Lilly started the day by reminding everyone of the spelling bee that afternoon.

"Raymond, is our superspeller ready to compete?" she asked.

Without thinking Raymond answered, "Sure, Daisy has been helping me practice."

Madison turned around in her seat so fast that she almost fell out of it. First she looked at Raymond and then at Daisy. Then she whispered something to Lizzie.

Raymond quietly said, "I'm sorry, Daisy. I didn't think it was a big deal."

Ms. Lilly started to talk about Valley Forge. She was writing some facts on the board, so Daisy wrote a note to Raymond that said: *Oh great! Everything is a big deal to Madison.*

Raymond was so bummed, he didn't even send the note back. After a while, Blanca pointed behind Daisy toward Raymond.

Turning slightly, Daisy could see that Raymond's head was on his desk. Either he had stayed up all night studying, or he was upset about the whole Madison thing. This was not the right frame of mind to be in for a contest like the spelling bee.

Madison was undoing all of Daisy's hard work. It had taken Daisy a week to get Raymond ready to lead their class to victory. It only took Madison one mean look to undo it all.

It was a long morning! Daisy slipped Raymond two more notes, but he didn't even lift his head to read them. Ms. Lilly seemed to be ignoring the fact that he wasn't participating in the discussion about geometry. Often Raymond didn't say anything, so maybe Ms. Lilly didn't notice.

The truth was that earlier in the year, Ms. Lilly had tried to catch Raymond off-guard several times. Each time, he was able to answer any question she asked.

One day he was playing cards during her lecture about Egyptian kings. When she called on him, he gave a lecture of his own with more facts than she had given. She decided he was actually supersmart and probably bored in class.

When the bell rang for lunch, Daisy tapped Raymond on the shoulder. "We better review your words at lunch," she said.

Raymond's head snapped up. "Okay," he said. Just like that, he was ready to go. Lunch was his best subject after all.

When they got to the cafeteria, Daisy suggested that she sit at the end of the table with Raymond where he usually sat alone. He just nodded.

Inside his head, he was having a party! The nicest girl in school was going to eat lunch with him. He wondered if anyone would notice.

Unfortunately, someone did! Raymond set his lunch tray on the table and Daisy scooted her lunch box down beside him. She always brought her lunch. Abuela fixed one every day for every one of the Martinez kids.

Daisy pulled out her lunch and the spelling bee practice book. Just as they got started, Madison and Lizzie stopped at the end of the table.

"Isn't this cute?" Madison teased. "Raymond and Daisy are quite the couple lately. Look at the busy bees pretending to study. Really, you don't need an excuse to sit together. You are probably secretly dating!"

Raymond turned as red as a tomato. Then he sneered, "Shut up, Madison! You don't even know what you're talking about. Daisy is my friend."

Daisy's mouth was still wide open waiting to say something, but suddenly she lost her words. Closing her mouth she turned to look at her friends at the other end of the table.

Blanca was trying to stand up, but DeShaye was pulling her back down to her seat. Blanca shouted, "This is war!"

Min came quietly to their end of the table and gave her own advice. "Success is the best revenge," she advised them.

Daisy nodded and began to call the spelling bee words again. But she was thinking that Madison had gone too far this time.

That afternoon the school auditorium was crowded and loud. The students all waited for the spelling bee to start.

Finally, Principal Donaldson welcomed them all to the Townsend Elementary Fourth-Grade Spelling Bee. He told them that the winner would be going to the citywide spelling bee.

Then all six of the contestants came out and sat on metal chairs on the stage. Daisy made sure she was in the front row to encourage Raymond. She gave him a quick thumbs-up.

At first, it seemed like no one would ever miss a word, but finally one by one they misspelled a word. Soon, only Raymond and a girl named Elizabeth were left.

It was Elizabeth's turn and Mr. Harrison, the spelling bee sponsor, called the word *chrysanthemum*. Elizabeth seemed to spell with confidence, but Daisy listened carefully to each letter. Daisy knew Elizabeth was wrong when she used a *u* instead of an *e* toward the end of the word.

Mr. Harrison announced, "I'm sorry, Elizabeth. That is incorrect. If Raymond can spell the word he will be our winner."

Daisy turned to Blanca whispering excitedly, "He knows this one!"

Raymond stepped up to the microphone confidently. He knew how to spell the word. He cleared his throat.

Daisy grabbed Blanca's hand and they both leaned forward. Quietly Blanca asked, "Are you sure he can spell it, Daisy?"

Daisy nodded a quick yes as Raymond began. He spoke slowly, "C-h-r-y-" he paused, "s-a-n," again a pause, "t-h-e-m-u-m." Then he shouted, "Chrysanthemum!"

Daisy and Blanca jumped up and down and hugged each other. Their whole class cheered for Raymond. Even Madison stood up.

Mr. Harrison shook Raymond's hand and gave him a huge, gold trophy and a giant, blue ribbon. Then all at once everyone seemed to be pushing out the door.

Raymond jumped off the stage and handed Daisy the blue ribbon. He said, "You deserve it! Thanks for being my coach!" He added, "I'm keeping the trophy though."

8

The War

All through history, wars were started over nothing. This war with Madison is really no different, Daisy thought. Madison's mean comments had prompted Blanca to declare war the day before at lunch. Today, her class was divided just like a battlefield.

There were fewer kids on Madison's side, but Daisy didn't like the tension in the room. To make matters worse, they had a substitute. Ms. Lilly would have known how to fix the problem. The sub didn't even realize anything was going on!

The substitute was old. Blanca guessed she was eighty. Her name was Ms. Nelson. Some of the kids called her No Nonsense Nelson.

Ms. Nelson had subbed at Townsend Elementary many times over the years. She didn't allow any talking, kept any notes she collected, and didn't give any hall passes!

During art Madison announced, "Raymond and Daisy are a couple—a couple of losers!"

Daisy turned and begged, "Please, Madison, can we just forget the whole thing? Raymond and I are just friends. If this war doesn't stop it will ruin our dance."

Lizzie replied for Madison, "Why should we care?"

Daisy explained that it was their dance too and they would only have one fourth-grade dance. This argument did not seem to stop Madison.

Before Daisy and her friends could pick up their lunch, Madison and her allies camped out at their usual table. This left Daisy and her friends trying to find a table with enough seats so they could sit together.

Scanning the cafeteria, Daisy could see that the tables were already full with only a few empty seats here and there. She took a deep breath and then suggested, "Maybe we should just sit on Raymond's end of the table. Mami says the best way to fight an enemy is to make them a friend."

Blanca stopped walking and stood in the center of the aisle. She thought it over and then finally turned toward their usual table. She reasoned, "Well, I guess either Madison will get madder or she'll get over it."

Everyone in Daisy's group sat down at "their" table. Madison shrieked, "Hey, those seats are saved!"

Raymond looked around the cafeteria. No one else was waiting to sit and everyone had a seat.

Min suggested, "Let's just pretend we don't hear her." It seemed like a good plan, so they all began eating their lunch and talking about the dance.

After a while DeShaye asked, "Madison, what does your dress look like?"

At first Madison ignored the question, but then she decided to answer DeShaye. She insisted that her dress would be the most fabulous one at the dance because it cost $200.

Daisy couldn't believe anyone would spend that much money on one outfit for a kid. Her dress and shoes together only cost $30 and she thought that was a whole lot of money.

Madison was giving all the details about her dress, gushing over a special designer label. Daisy took a deep breath. She smiled nervously and then complimented Madison.

"Your dress will be absolutely dy-no-mite!" Daisy said.

Madison's eyes popped open wide and then narrowed. She probably thought Daisy was up to something, but all Daisy wanted was to end the war so everyone could get back to being normal again.

Madison managed to stammer out, "Thanks, I guess." Then just like air whooshing out of a balloon, the tension seemed to leave the table.

For the next ten minutes everyone seemed to be over it. But then Madison tried to stir them all up again.

"I think we should make everyone come to the dance with a date," Madison insisted.

Daisy wondered what to say. She and Madison had had this same conversation last week. They had finally agreed that everyone should be able to come to the dance, date or no date.

Mami and Papi would not allow Daisy to go on a date, even to a dance! Her parents were very old-fashioned that way. Actually Daisy was glad, because she didn't feel ready to go on a date. Dating boys was kind of scary still.

That's when Raymond's eye caught Daisy's. He looked quickly away. Maybe he would ask her to the dance tomorrow. He didn't want to ask her in front of everyone.

Finally Daisy said, "Madison, you know we already agreed about the whole date thing."

Madison and her friends seemed to have moved on to talking about the end of the year picnic. Looking bored Madison responded, "Whatever, Daisy!"

Just like that the war was over. Daisy took a deep breath. Sometimes fourth grade was just too much drama!

9

Decorating Divas

"I can't believe tomorrow is finally Friday!" Blanca exclaimed. They were on their way to the gym to decorate for the dance. The decorations committee had asked for more volunteers, so several kids were meeting them to help.

Everything was already made, so it would only take about an hour if enough kids showed up. Amber was skipping she was so excited.

Raymond was carrying a stack of boxes. He asked, "Can someone steer me in the right direction? I can't see."

Blanca grabbed his arm and guided him to the gym doors. Some of the other boys were bringing in boxes, too. Min and DeShaye had huge bags full of silver balloons. The custodians brought in two tall ladders.

The new helpers all stood in the center of the room looking around. "Some of you can decorate the ceiling if you are not afraid of heights," Daisy said. "Some can work on the tables. And some of you can put up posters."

The boys quickly volunteered to hang the disco balls. They would also tie the balloons and streamers along the edge of the basketball court.

Raymond asked, "Daisy, what are you going to work on?"

Daisy was so distracted by everything that needed to be done. She suggested, "Raymond, help me with the tables. Okay?" He was right behind her as she called out directions to DeShaye and Min sticking posters on the walls.

Daisy began to shake out the tie-dyed tablecloths they had gotten at the party store. Raymond helped her place them on the tables. Daisy noticed he was really fidgety and kept looking around.

When they got to last table they were all the way across the room from everyone else. Raymond said, "Daisy . . ."

She waited for him to ask her if they were almost done. He said her name again and looked like he might be sick. Then in a big rush he blurted, "Daisy, please be my date for the dance!"

His face was red, but he smiled, because she was smiling. Daisy was thinking that Blanca had been right all along. *What could she say?* She didn't want to have a date for the dance.

Finally she said, "Raymond, I don't . . ."

Holding up his hands he begged, "Don't say no! You know I really like you, Daisy."

Other kids were starting to look in their direction. Daisy leaned forward whispering, "Raymond, I like you too. But my parents won't let me have a date for the dance, so why don't we go together as friends."

Raymond grinned and shouted, "Yes!"

Blanca's curiosity had her heading in their direction. When she got close she asked, "What's up?"

Raymond said, "Ask Daisy."

Blanca looked to Daisy. "Nothing really, I'll tell you about it later," Daisy said. Blanca made a remark about being the last person to know anything.

Everyone kept up the pace. Before long, the room looked ready for everyone to boogie on down the next night.

Looking around DeShaye commented, "We are the decorating divas!"

Raymond and the other boys acted insulted. Raymond countered, "We are the decorating dudes!"

The room filled with laughter and shouts as everyone filed out to go home. When Daisy got home she just had to tell Mami and Abuela about the decorations. Paola wanted to hear, too.

While they were getting dinner ready, all of the Martinez women chatted happily about the dance. Even Carmen cooed from her highchair.

After she finished describing all of the posters, disco balls, and tablecloths, Daisy began to set the table for dinner. She kind of wished her mother and grandmother could come to the dance to see all of her hard work for themselves.

Daisy decided not to tell Mami or Abuela about Raymond asking her to the dance. It was kind of fun to have a secret of her own. She was still deciding whether or not to tell Blanca.

The kitchen smelled delicious as Abuela lifted lids and stirred pots. Daisy was starving! All that work made her hungry.

Paola vowed, "When I am in fourth grade, I'm going to be class president and go to the dance just like you, Daisy."

This made Daisy giggle. Daisy felt *orgullosa* that Paola wanted to be like her. She warned Paola, "It's a lot more work than you think!"

Soon everyone was gathered around the table. The big bowls of hot food went round and round as everyone had seconds and her brothers ate thirds.

Papi reminded Manuel and Diego it was the boy's night to do the dishes. Abuela reminded Daisy it was time to hem her dress for the dance. They went to Mami's room, because she had a tall mirror.

Daisy slipped the dress on and stood on a stool so her dress could be pinned up for hemming. They couldn't talk because Abuela had the pins clenched between her lips. She looked liked a crazy vampire!

Every now and then, Abuela pointed in the direction she wanted Daisy to turn. She quickly slipped the tiny silver pins into the fabric. Later she would hem the dress by hand instead of using her sewing machine.

When the last pin was in place, Daisy turned to look in the mirror and gasped. The dress fit her perfectly! She bragged, "Abuela, no store-bought dress could ever fit this good."

Daisy went to her room to do her homework. In no time at all, Abuela was finished. She called, "Mi ja, come try on your dress again."

Daisy closed her history book and went back to Mami's room. She slipped on the dress and couldn't believe that her grandmother had made a mistake. It was too long!

Daisy wondered if she should say anything. But before she could point out the problem, her Abuela noticed, too.

"Daisy, go get your sandals. I made it a little long so it would not be too short with your shoes on," Abuela explained.

Once she returned with her sandals on, Abuela suggested she model for Mami and Papi. Daisy took the band out of her hair and fluffed out her braid. Her hair looked like a black lace shawl against the colorful dress.

Daisy looked in the mirror one last time before going downstairs. She thought the dress made her look very pretty. It was sleeveless with a round neckline and full skirt.

She cried, *"Gracias, Gracias. ¡Me encanta, Abuela!"*

Everyone in the living room was watching television when Daisy slipped quietly into the room. Manuel noticed Daisy first. "Hey, you look pretty!" he exclaimed.

Mami jumped up and came over to Daisy saying, "You look just like a disco queen. You will be the most beautiful girl at the dance."

Paola circled around her sister begging to try on the dress even if it was too big for her.

Papi came over and bowed. "May I have this dance?" he asked. Then he twirled her around the living room.

Mami asked Manuel to dance. Diego asked Paola. Abuela spun Carmen around the room. Laughter and giggling filled the tiny space as the couples bumped into each other.

One by one the couples got tired of spinning until they were all sitting again. They all complained about being worn-out from dancing.

"Perfect timing! It's bedtime now, " Papi decided.

10

Fourth Grade Fever

The next morning at school, the fourth-grade hall was buzzing with dance talk. Blanca kept bugging Daisy about what had gone on in the gym with Raymond.

"It didn't look or sound like nothing," Blanca tried again. "I've been telling you all year long that he likes you a lot."

Daisy's pink cheeks were giving her away. "Tell me!" Blanca insisted.

Daisy hesitated for a minute, then she dragged Blanca into the girl's restroom. She shut the door, then she demanded that Blanca promise she wouldn't tell anyone. Blanca agreed instantly!

"Okay, you were right. Raymond does like me," Daisy admitted. "And he asked me to be his date for the dance."

Blanca started squealing and jumping up and down. Daisy tried to shush her, but she was too excited.

"Tell me everything, every word Raymond said," Blanca begged. Suddenly she looked upset. "Wait! You have a date and I'm going to be all alone!"

Daisy explained that she had told Raymond no, adding, "You know Mami and Papi won't let me date until I'm older." Daisy assured her they were going to go as friends, just friends. She could tell her BFF was relieved!

In room 210 it was the last day of their Revolutionary War unit. Ms. Lilly was back and she was wearing a long dress with an apron and a puffy white hat on her head. She was a colonial lady. On her desk was a silver tea set.

"Well, my superstar students," Ms. Lilly announced, "since today is our last day in George Washington's time, I decided to have a tea party. You can consider it a Boston Tea Party, but just don't throw any tea."

It was good to have a fun party. Ms. Lilly was dashing around the room pouring tea. Finally she asked, "Who needs more tea?"

When no one replied, she set her teapot down. Blanca said, "I feel sorry for Min and DeShaye. They're having a test today on the Revolutionary War."

Raymond added, "We're lucky. We have the best teacher in the whole school. I like projects better than tests, and so does Ms. Lilly."

Once they finished the tea, they were off to art and then to lunch. All of the kids were talking about the dance. To Daisy's surprise, they were all planning to come.

DeShaye bragged, "Devon and his dad are picking me up, just like a real date." The rest of the girls were perfectly happy to be going to the dance together!

Raymond shared his chips with Daisy and Blanca tried not to look in their direction. She would rather die than give away Daisy's secret. From their talk in the girls' room Blanca could tell her friend actually liked Raymond back.

Min hardly ate two bites of her fried rice. "I'm too excited to eat!" she blurted out. That's when Raymond asked if he could have the rest of her lunch.

Finally, the afternoon bell rang and the fourth graders rushed home to get ready for the dance. Daisy, Blanca, and Raymond made one more visit to the gym to make sure everything was ready.

When she opened the door, Daisy gasped! All of their silver balloons were making a blanket on the gym floor. The helium had slowly seeped out overnight.

Blanca moaned, "What can we do now?"

Raymond headed for the door. Daisy called, "Raymond, where are you going?" He didn't even stop to answer, he just shouted over his shoulder, "To get Ms. Lilly!"

Minutes later both Raymond and Ms. Lilly appeared in the doorway. "Oh my! This will never do," their teacher insisted, shaking her head.

She told them that she could get Mr. Harrison to pick up some balloons in his van. But they would have to arrive before the dance to redecorate.

Blanca said, "I can't come early. My dad gets off work late tonight and he is bringing me when he gets home."

Ms. Lilly's eyes twinkled as she announced, "It will just be Raymond and Daisy then."

Raymond didn't mind at all. More time with Daisy sounded just fine with him. They were riding to the dance together anyway. Papi had agreed to pick up Raymond.

Ms. Lilly looked around the gym. She exclaimed, "Daisy, other than the balloon mishap, you and your committees have done a spectacular job. It looks just like a disco in here!"

Later that night, Daisy and Papi picked up Raymond at his house. He quickly jumped in the backseat with Daisy. When they got to the school, he jumped out and ran around to open the car door for her.

Papi said, "Raymond, you have excellent manners! I'll pick you both up right here at nine o'clock when the dance ends."

Inside the gym, Raymond got the ladder so he could climb up and tie the new silver balloons in just the right spot. Daisy carefully handed him bunches of balloons.

In no time at all the entire place looked perfect. They sat at a table talking until the rest of the kids arrived.

The boys in the band came in dragging their guitar cases and their drums. Jason was testing the sound system. Then they started to warm up by playing a slow song.

Raymond stood up and bowed. He said, "Daisy, can I please have this dance?" Sometimes he was really sweet.

She replied, "Okay." While they danced, Raymond told Daisy that she was going to be the most beautiful girl at the dance. Raymond

was a good dancer. He didn't step on her feet once!

It was almost seven when DeShaye and Devon came in with a bunch of kids behind them.

Raymond went to help Eric start the black lights. Genny and the girls were setting out punch and brownies. Lots of couples were hanging around the edges of the dance floor, but no one was dancing.

DeShaye shouted, "Hey, let's get this party started!" She pulled Devon out on floor and started to boogie. Min, Blanca, and some of the girls got out on the dance floor, too.

Daisy was quietly taking in the scene. Her fourth-grade year had been great, but she was a little sad that it was almost over. She remembered going on field trips and the fall festival. She had grown up a lot this year and she realized it was a good thing, because next year she was going to be in middle school!

Spanish Glossary

abuela – grandmother

bueno – good

Dejen en paz su hermana – Leave your sister in peace

Estas loco – You're crazy

gracias – thank you

Madison es una bebe grande – Madison is a big baby

¡Me encanta! – It's enchanting!

mi amor – my love

mi ja – my dear

orgullosa – proud

pan dulce – sweet bread

¿Que color era? – What color was it?

sí – yes